W9-AJS-432

Welcome to Penguin Young Readers! As parents and educators, you know that each child develops at his or her own pace—in terms of speech, critical thinking, and, of course, reading. Penguin Young Readers recognizes this fact. As a result, each Penguin Young Readers book is assigned a traditional easy-to-read level (1–4) as well as a Guided Reading Level (A–P). Both of these systems will help you choose the right book for your child. Please refer to the back of each book for specific leveling information. Penguin Young Readers features esteemed authors and illustrators, stories about favorite characters, fascinating nonfiction, and more!

Ant Plays Bear

LEVEL **3**

GUIDED READING LEVEL **J**

This book is perfect for a **Transitional Reader** who:
- can read multisyllable and compound words;
- can read words with prefixes and suffixes;
- is able to identify story elements (beginning, middle, end, plot, setting, characters, problem, solution); and
- can understand different points of view.

Here are some **activities** you can do during and after reading this book:
- Venn Diagrams: The boys in this book are brothers. Think about how they are alike and how they are different. On a separate sheet of paper, draw a Venn diagram. Write the character traits that are specific to each brother in the parts of the circles that don't touch. Write the character traits they share in the space where the circles overlap.
- Creative Writing: In "When Ant Grows Up," Ant and his brother talk about what they'd like to be when they grow up. What would you like to be when you grow up? Write a paragraph explaining why.

Remember, sharing the love of reading with a child is the best gift you can give!

—Bonnie Bader, EdM
   Penguin Young Readers program

*Penguin Young Readers are leveled by independent reviewers applying the standards developed by Irene Fountas and Gay Su Pinnell in *Matching Books to Readers: Using Leveled Books in Guided Reading*, Heinemann, 1999.

Penguin Young Readers
Published by the Penguin Group
Penguin Group (USA) Inc., 375 Hudson Street, New York, New York 10014, USA
Penguin Group (Canada), 90 Eglinton Avenue East, Suite 700, Toronto, Ontario M4P 2Y3, Canada
(a division of Pearson Penguin Canada Inc.)
Penguin Books Ltd, 80 Strand, London WC2R 0RL, England
Penguin Ireland, 25 St Stephen's Green, Dublin 2, Ireland (a division of Penguin Books Ltd)
Penguin Group (Australia), 707 Collins Street, Melbourne, Victoria 3008, Australia
(a division of Pearson Australia Group Pty Ltd)
Penguin Books India Pvt Ltd, 11 Community Centre, Panchsheel Park, New Delhi—110 017, India
Penguin Group (NZ), 67 Apollo Drive, Rosedale, Auckland 0632, New Zealand
(a division of Pearson New Zealand Ltd)
Penguin Books (South Africa), Rosebank Office Park, 181 Jan Smuts Avenue,
Parktown North 2193, South Africa
Penguin China, B7 Jiaming Center, 27 East Third Ring Road North,
Chaoyang District, Beijing 100020, China

Penguin Books Ltd, Registered Offices: 80 Strand, London WC2R 0RL, England

Text copyright © 1997 by Betsy Byars. Illustrations copyright © 1997 by Marc Simont. All rights reserved.
First published in 1997 by Viking, an imprint of Penguin Group (USA) Inc. Published in a Puffin
Easy-to-Read edition in 1999. Published in 2013 by Penguin Young Readers, an imprint of Penguin Group
(USA) Inc., 345 Hudson Street, New York, New York 10014. Manufactured in China.

The Library of Congress has cataloged the Viking edition
under the following Control Number: 96048278

ISBN 978-0-14-130351-2   10 9 8 7 6 5 4 3 2 1

PENGUIN YOUNG READERS

LEVEL
TRANSITIONAL
READER
3

APR   2013

Ant Plays Bear

by Betsy Byars
illustrated by Marc Simont

Penguin Young Readers
An Imprint of Penguin Group (USA) Inc.

Chapter 1
Ant Plays Bear

"Let's play . . ."

Anthony said slowly.

He stopped to think.

He started again.

"Let's play . . ."

He stopped to think.

"Let's play . . ."

This time his thinking worked.

"Let's play Bear."

"Oh, I don't know," I said.

"I'm tired.

I've been raking leaves."

Ant said, "Please, please, please,

please—"

"Oh, all right," I said.

"How do you play?"

"One of us is the bear," Ant said.

"The other one is the person."

"What does the bear do?" I asked.

"Does he run around and climb trees?

Or does he lie down in a cave?

If he lies down in a cave.

I will be the bear."

"Yes!" said the Ant.

"I will make the cave."

He got a blanket.

He put it over a table.

He said, "Go inside."

I crawled in.

I lay down.

I said, "This is it?

This is the game?"

"Yes," said the Ant.

"While you are lying there,

I come along.

I am the person.

I am humming and picking flowers.

I don't know you are in there."

I waited in the cave.

I was bored.

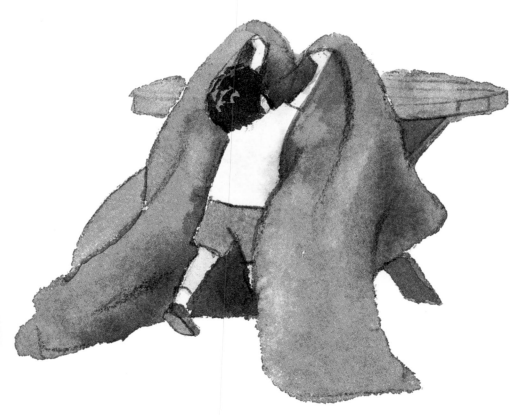

I heard Ant coming along, humming.

I went, *"Grrrrr."*

The humming stopped.

Ant said, "I heard something.

Did you hear something?

I heard something like growls."

I went, *"Grrrrr."*

Ant said, "Is that you growling?

It sounded like a real bear."

A real bear!

I began to like this game.

"Grrrrrrr."

Ant said, "Was that you?

Did you just go *grrrrrr*?"

I went, *"Grrrrrrr!"*

Ant said, "I'm not playing anymore.

I do not like this game."

"Grrrrrrr!"

Ant said, "Stop that!

I am not playing!"

He pulled off the blanket.

He looked at me.

I looked at the Ant.

I went, *"Grrrr."*

He said, "I knew it was you.

I knew it all the time.

But let's not play Bear anymore.

All right?"

"All right," I said.

Chapter 2
My Dog, Ant

Ant was down on the floor.

I said, "Get up, Ant."

Ant said, *"Bowwow."*

I said, "Are you being a dog again?"

"Bowwow."

"Well, stop it.

My new friend is coming over.

I don't want him to think

my brother is a dog."

Ant sat up and begged.

"Bowwow."

"That is not funny, Ant.

Now, stop it," I said.

I went to the window to look

for my friend.

The Ant came, too.

He sat up.

"Bowwow."

I yelled, "Mom!

Ant is acting like a dog again,

and my friend is coming over.

Make him stop."

My mother came in.

She said, "What a nice dog.

I bet he wants a pat on the head."

"Bowwow."

She patted him.

"And a cookie?"

"Bowwow."

"Well, come on into the kitchen."

Ant started into the kitchen.

The doorbell rang.

Ant turned around.

He ran to the door.

"Bowwow wow wow wow!"

I opened the door.

My friend came in.

He said, "Who's that?"

I said, "My brother.

He's being a dog."

We went outside.

The Ant came, too.

My friend said,

"You know what I do

to get rid of my dog?"

I said, "What?"

He said, "I get a stick

and throw it."

He found a stick.

Ant said, *"Bowwow wow."*

"I throw the stick—"

He got ready to throw it.

"—the dog runs after it,

and I run away and hide.

When the dog comes back,

he can't find me.

It's fun."

He looked at the Ant.

"You want a stick?

Run after the stick!"

My friend threw the stick.

Ant got up.

But he did not go after the stick.

He walked into the house.

He shut the door.

"Ant, come on back.

Ant!" I called.

"Let him go," my friend said.

My friend and I played for an hour,

but I did not have fun.

After he went home,

I went into the house.

The Ant was looking at a book.

I said, "Ant?"

Ant said, "That is really mean,

to throw a stick for a dog

and run away.

I am glad I am not a dog."

"I am, too, Ant."

"And if I ever have a dog,

I will never do that," said Ant.

"I won't, either, Ant," I said.

"Promise?"

"I promise."

"Me too," said the Ant.

Chapter 3
Something at the Window

Tap tap.

"There is someone tapping
on our window," Ant said.

"Ant, I am trying to get to sleep."

"Me too, but I can't.

Someone is tapping on the window."

I said, "Ant, be real.

Our room is on the second floor.

No one could tap on our window."

"A giant could," Ant said.

"There are no giants," I said.

"Well, someone with very long legs."

"Everyone with very long legs
is playing basketball.
Now, Ant, go to sleep," I said.

"Will you look?" Ant asked.

"What?"

"Will you pull back the curtain
and look?"

"Then will you go to sleep?" I said.

23

"Yes," said Ant.

I went to the window.

I pulled back the curtain.

"There is nobody there," I said.

"Then what is going *tap tap* like that?"

"The tree.

The tree!" I said.

"The wind is blowing.

A branch of the tree is tapping

at the window."

I got back into bed.

"Good night, Ant."

"See, I was right," Ant said.

"There was somebody

tapping on the window."

"A tree!

A tree!" I said.

"A tree is not somebody!

"Now this is the last time

I'm saying this.

Good night, Ant!"

"Good night."

Then Ant said softly,

"Good night, tree."

Tap Tap.

Chapter 4
When Ant Grows Up

"I know what I'm going to be
when I grow up," Ant said.

"What?" I said.

"Guess."

I thought about it.

I said, "A fireman."

"And ride on fire trucks?" Ant asked.

"And put out fires?"

"Yes," I said.

"I would like to do those things.

But that is not what I am going to be.

Guess again," said Ant.

I said, "A farmer."

"And grow stuff?" Ant asked.

"And ride on tractors?

And take care of cows?"

"Yes," I said.

"I would like to do those things.

But that is not what I am going to be."

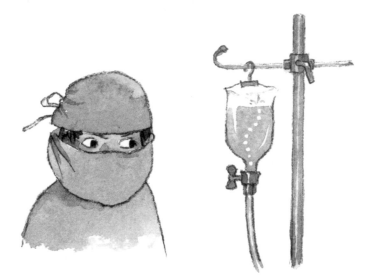

I said, "A doctor."

"And make people well?" Ant asked.

"So there will be no more sick
people?"

"Yes," I said.

"I would like to do that.
But you still have to guess again,"
said Ant.

I said, "I am tired of guessing.
I give up."

"You can't give up.

You have to guess," said Ant.

I said, "Give me a hint."

Ant thought about it.

He said, "Here is the hint.

I am going to be the same as Dad."

"You're going to be

a teacher, Ant?" I said.

He said, "No!

Not a teacher!

I am going to be a man.

And after I get to be a man,

then maybe I will be a fireman,

or a farmer, or a doctor,

or a teacher."

"Good thinking," I said.

He said, "What are you going to be?"

I said, "The same thing—a man."

He said, "We're going to be the same thing!

We're going to be the exact same thing.

Mom and Dad have to hear this!"

"Ant," I said,

"it can wait until we get home.

Trust me.

It can wait."

"Oh, all right," said Ant,

"but I want to be the one to tell them."

"You will be, Ant," I said.

"You will."